DAISY
The Diabetic Donkey

JESSICA LEWIS

Balboa Press books may be ordered through booksellers or by contacting:

Balboa Press
A Division of Hay House
1663 Liberty Drive
Bloomington, IN 47403
www.balboapress.com
844–682–1282

ISBN: 979–8–7652–3516–4 (sc)
ISBN: 979–8–7652–3517–1 (e)

Library of Congress Control Number: 2022918229

Print information available on the last page.

Balboa Press rev. date: 10/26/2022

BALBOA.PRESS
A DIVISION OF HAY HOUSE

DAISY
The Diabetic Donkey

This story was inspired by all of Jess's T1D
warriors, whom she's had the pleasure
of navigating their journeys with

Most everyone loves donuts, danishes, and chocolate cake. But, to Daisy, there's much more at stake.

Daisy is a special donkey, with a unique condition. Her Type One Diabetes can often put her in a tough position.

Too many sweets like these can make her feel very sick. When this happens, Daisy must act quick! This condition isn't contagious like the cold or flu. Let me break it down for you.

Type One Diabetes can make Daisy an interesting client; due to her pancreas that can act very defiant.

The pancreas makes something called insulin that gives the body energy. Because Daisy has Type One Diabetes, it's not that easy.

When Daisy eats, her body cannot handle the sugar. With the help of her friend Omnipod, her days are less of a bugger.

Omnipod sits on her arm, feeding her insulin all day long. With all of this extra help, Dasiy feels STRONG.

When Daisy's Diabetes gets her feeling sick, she can check her sugar levels with one little prick!

Between 80 and 120 are what her levels should be, but sometimes those levels are off, you see.

When Daisy's body does not make enough insulin for sugary foods, high blood sugars may cause slight changes to her moods.

When her sugar levels rise, tummy trouble or thirst may come as a slight surprise.

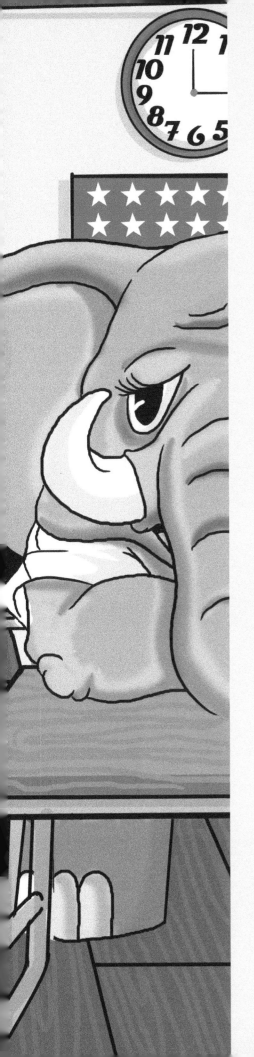

When daisy's blood sugar is high, dangerous ketones sometimes tend to arise.

Drinking water keeps Daisy from getting sick. Then, she waits for the clock to tick..

After time passes; Daisy uses the restroom--where those pesky ketones get flushed down, ZOOM!

For Daisy's high blood sugar to come down to a normal level, insulin in her Omnnipod and exercise can make it settle!

Anytime she gets the chance, she likes to get up and DANCE!

If Daisy's blood sugar drops low, she can often feel very dizzy or slow.

To make sure her levels are up to par, she eats a special treat, like a candy bar!

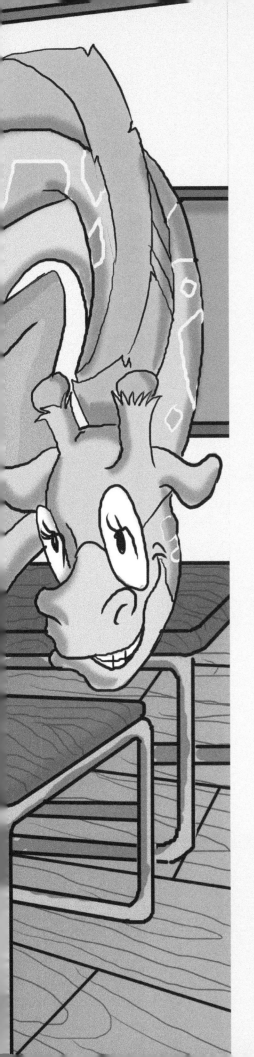

Daisy is just like everyone else. She just has to take extra good care of herself.

Whether Daisy is dancing or enjoying a sweet treat, keeping her levels steady is actually pretty neat!

HEE-HAW!

22

Lightning Source UK Ltd.
Milton Keynes UK
UKHW020208131222
413813UK00008B/166